y was white, with lig
d brown spots on her
xe freckles. Her ears kly
a floppy that they flapp up and
wn as she tumbled around in her
ket. She jumped up as soon as she
ted Naima, and her feathery brown
aced from side-to-side excitedly.
aima knelt down at the wire and put
her fingers up against it for Suzy to sniff.
Suzy pushed her wet black nose up to her
hand, and put her head on one side,
watching Naima with her twinkly black
eyes. "Hi!" Naima whispered softly.

www.kidsatrandomhouse.co.uk

www.battersea.org.uk

Have you read all these books in the **Battersea Dogs & Cats Home** series?

SUZY'S story

by

Sarah Hawkins

Illustrated by Artful Doodlers

Puzzle illustrations by Jason Chapman

RED FOX

BATTERSEA DOGS AND CATS HOME: SUZY'S STORY
A RED FOX BOOK 978 1 849 41481 4

First published in Great Britain by Red Fox,
an imprint of Random House Children's Books
A Random House Group Company

This edition published 2012

1 3 5 7 9 10 8 6 4 2

The Random House Group Limited supports the Forest Stewardship Council (FSC®), the leading international forest certification organization. Our books carrying the FSC label are printed on FSC®-certified paper. FSC is the only forest certification scheme endorsed by the leading environmental organizations, including Greenpeace. Our paper procurement policy can be found at www.randomhouse.co.uk/environment.

Set in 13/20 Stone Informal

Red Fox Books are published by Random House Children's Books,
61–63 Uxbridge Road, London W5 5SA

www.**kidsatrandomhouse**.co.uk
www.**totallyrandombooks**.co.uk

Addresses for companies within The Random House Group Limited
can be found at: www.randomhouse.co.uk/offices.htm

THE RANDOM HOUSE GROUP Limited Reg. No. 954009

A CIP catalogue record for this book is available from the British Library.

Printed and bound by CPI Group (UK)
Ltd, Croydon, CR0 4YY

Turn to page 91 for lots
of information on
Battersea Dogs & Cats Home,
plus some cool activities!

Meet the stars of the Battersea Dogs & Cats Home series to date . . .

Angel
Cosmo
Alfie
Buddy and Holly
Coco
Petal
Suzy
Bertie

Double Trouble

"One and two and three and four," Naima Sanhi chanted as she practised her dance steps. She was getting out of breath, but it was a nice feeling as her feet stepped nimbly in time next to her sister's. "Now for the big finish . . ." Naima paused as music started coming from Mina's schoolbag.

"Hang on, that's my phone." Mina

grabbed it and rushed out of the lounge.

"Mina . . . we're rehearsing!" Naima called, but her sister was already gone. Naima sighed and turned to her best friend Tammy, who was watching from the sofa with her Jack Russell terrier, Archie, sat on her lap.

"More! More!" Tammy cheered and clapped as she pretended to be a whole audience. "Whoooo! We want the world-famous Sanhi sisters!"

"Woof! Woof!" Archie agreed.

Naima flopped down next to Tammy and stroked Archie's ears. Tammy was always so nice about her dancing, but sometimes she got too over-excited! "We're not *world-famous*," she giggled.

"Well, not *yet*." Tammy smiled. "But once you and Mina win the Tween Time competition you will be. And I can say I'm the best friend of Naima Sanhi, and her biggest fan! Aren't you nervous though?" Tammy asked seriously. "Tween Time is so much bigger than all the other contests you've done."

Naima nodded. "And this is only the audition. If we get through then the real contest is in a month's time."

"You'll get through, I know you will." Tammy smiled.

Naima wasn't so sure. She couldn't actually believe that she and Mina were going to be performing in front of so many people. Dancing felt like something they did for fun, not to get famous. Her big sister had always loved Indian Bollywood musicals, and she'd been making Naima learn dance routines from the films since they were both tiny. One of Mum's favourite pictures was of them both as little kids, dressed up in a pair of old curtains, performing for all their aunties and uncles. One of the best things about coming from a big Indian family

was that there were always lots of people to make up an audience!

Soon Naima and Mina were performing a dance at every family gathering, and then one of their aunties had entered them into a talent competition – and they'd won! After that they'd started rehearsing seriously, and Mum and Nani had made them proper matching gold-and-pink costumes, with jingly headdresses and bangles and everything. They'd won lots of contests, and even been asked to perform at the opening of their town's new library in front of Princess Anne. Tammy had been really impressed that Naima had met a real-life princess!

Naima was always anxious before a performance, but she was feeling especially nervous this time. Not only was Tween Time the biggest competition so far, but Mina hadn't wanted to practise as much recently. Normally she was the one nagging Naima to go over their steps, but now she was always on the computer or on the phone to her friends. There were only two days to go until the audition, and it felt like they still had lots of work to do.

"Earth to Naima!" Tammy interrupted her thoughts.

Naima shook her head, sending her long, dark hair flying. "Sorry!" She grinned. "I was just thinking. I am a bit nervous, I suppose. But we just need to rehearse more. After all – practise makes perfect!"

But that night, things got a lot worse. When Naima and Dad got back from walking Tammy and Archie home, they could hear cross voices inside.

"You're not just letting your sister down, you're letting the whole family down!" Mum yelled.

Mina was sitting on the sofa, still wearing her dancing costume. "I don't want to do it!" she shouted back. "I just want to be a normal teenager!

All that stuff was fine when I was a kid, but I'm not doing it anymore! Sherry's having a party on Saturday and I'm going to that instead." She stomped upstairs, not even looking at Naima as she passed.

Mum gave a cross sigh and sat down on the sofa. Naima could feel a funny cold feeling spreading to her toes. "Doesn't Mina want to perform with me?" she asked.

Mum opened her arms and Naima went to snuggle up next to her.

"It'll be ok, my *beti.*" She hugged her. "She'll change her mind. She's just turning into a teenager, that's all. She loves dancing with you really."

Naima wasn't sure – she knew how stubborn her big sister was. If Mina said she wouldn't do it then she meant it. And without her sister . . . the double act was over.

Bad News and Good News

Mina stayed in her room all evening and didn't even come down for dinner. After she'd eaten, Naima crept up to take her a cup of tea and some of her favourite *petha* sweets. She tapped lightly on her bedroom door.

"What?" Mina called crossly. Naima edged the door open. "Oh, it's you." Mina sighed. "Sorry, I thought Mum was coming to have a go at me again."

Naima shook her head. "I just brought you some tea." She looked at her sister. Mina's hair was just as long as hers, even though she desperately wanted to get it cut. Mum had said they needed to look the same for the show. Mina gave a big sigh.

"It's not that I don't like dancing with you, Nai," she started. "It's just . . . I want to do other things too. And not being able to go to this party was the last straw." She looked at Mina earnestly. "Do you understand?"

Naima nodded sadly. She did understand, but she wished Mina still wanted to do their act. "Mum's already told me that we'll change the routine so I can do it by myself," she told her sister. "But it won't be the same."

"It'll be even better, Nai," Mina smiled. "I'll help you rehearse."

Naima grinned. "Can we go through it now? I'm not too sure about the second spin . . ."

"Sure!" Mina replied. "Although not *right* now, I promised Sherry I'd call her to talk about party decorations."

"OK," Naima sighed.

"I promise we'll do it later," Mina said, picking up the phone.

Naima went into her room and curled up on her bed. As she thought about doing the routine on her own, she couldn't stop a tear from trickling down her cheek. She brushed it away crossly. *It just wasn't fair! Why did things have to change?*

*

The next morning, Naima's eyes were tired and sore and she felt like she had a heavy lump in her tummy. She got dressed in her school uniform slowly.

When she went down to breakfast, Mina just grabbed some toast and rushed out to catch her bus. Mum tutted as Mina flew past. "You'll get indigestion!" she yelled. Then she turned back to Naima and sighed.

Dad put his arm round Mum's waist. "She's a teenager," he soothed her. "She wants to be out with her friends. You remember what we were like, Mala." He laughed, kissing the top of her head. "But if Mina's not going to be around as much, I was thinking it might be time to look for a *new* member of the family."

Naima looked up from her cereal, puzzled.

"Don't look at me." Mum shrugged. "I haven't a clue what he's talking about."

"I'm talking about getting a pet!" Dad laughed. "We always said we'd get one when the girls were older, and we never did. It would be nice company for Naima. We could get a cat, or a rabbit—"

"Or a puppy!" Naima interrupted. "*Please* can we get a puppy! I always help take Archie for walks when I visit Tammy."

Mum and Dad looked at each other. "It would be nice to have someone to go

on walks with."

Dad raised an eyebrow at Mum. "It's OK with me, if it's OK with your mother."

Naima jumped up and grabbed her mum's hands so hard that her bangles jingled. "Please, Mum! Please, please, please!" she pleaded.

Mum paused. "Are you sure you wouldn't rather have something smaller – like a guinea pig? Puppies take up a lot of time, you know, and you're already so busy with school and your shows . . ."

"A guinea pig?" Naima screwed her face up. "I'm not too busy for a puppy, honestly I'm not. We can walk him before school and I'll play with him after I rehearse. And I want one sooooo badly! Please, Mum, please!"

Mum smiled. "You look so happy that I can't say no!"

"Really?" Naima shrieked, jumping up and down in excitement.

"We'll go to an animal sanctuary and get a rescue dog," Dad suggested.

"Battersea Dogs & Cats Home isn't too far away, and they have lots of dogs that are all looking for a family to love them. We can go up there on Saturday."

"*This* Saturday – like *tomorrow*?" Naima breathed. *Were her parents really talking about going to pick a puppy* tomorrow?

"But what about the show?" Mum reminded them. "It's the audition tomorrow, don't forget."

"If we leave early enough in the morning we'll be back in plenty of time for the audition," Dad said. "What do you think, Naima? You'll have to practise lots tonight after school so you're all ready."

"I will!" Naima promised happily. She couldn't believe it. She'd been so miserable when she woke up, but this was turning out to be the best day of her life!

Suzy the Springer Spaniel

The next day, Naima got up bright and early to practise her new routine before they set off to Battersea Dogs & Cats Home. She enjoyed bouncing through the twists and spins, and she was too excited about meeting her puppy to feel nervous about the audition that afternoon.

"If you dance like that later, you're

bound to get through," Mum said, encouragingly. "I've never seen you with such a big smile."

"I was thinking about the puppy!" Naima giggled.

Even Mina seemed excited about getting a pet – although she decided to go round to Sherry's house to try on outfits for their party that evening, rather than come up to London with them. Naima was so confused about her sister – how could choosing clothes be more exciting than choosing a puppy?

When Mum, Dad and Naima arrived at Battersea, they were met by a nice lady called Annie, who asked them questions about their lifestyle and what type of dog they were looking for. Soon it was time for the bit Naima had been waiting for – meeting the dogs! Naima held her breath as Annie led them through a long corridor lined with doggy pens. Inside each one was a different dog.

Naima wandered down the corridor to look at all the dogs, reading the nametags that were attached to the kennel.

"Aw, look at this one," Mum said as she and Dad stopped to look at a black Labrador. It wagged its tail at them and gnawed at a chew toy. Naima went to go and join them – but then she saw Suzy.

She was white, with light-brown ears and brown spots on her fur that looked just like freckles. Her ears were so crinkly and floppy that they flapped up and down as she tumbled around in her basket. She jumped up as soon as she spotted Naima, and her feathery brown tail raced from side-to-side excitedly.

Naima knelt down at the wire and put her fingers up against it for Suzy to sniff. Suzy pushed her wet black nose up to her hand and put her head on one side, watching Naima with her twinkly black eyes.

"Hi!" Naima whispered softly.

"Ooh, who's this?" Mum exclaimed as the others crowded round to look at Suzy.

"Oh, Mum," Naima sighed, "she's the most beautiful puppy I've ever seen!"

"She's a very pretty dog," Annie agreed. "And she's very energetic, too. Springer Spaniels make really good family dogs. "

Annie opened the kennel door for Naima to enter. Suzy padded over and jumped up at Naima, standing up on her hind legs. Then, as if she knew she had an audience, she turned round in a circle and gave a happy "Yap!"

"She's dancing!" Naima giggled.

"Oh look," Mum laughed. "She's a little performer – just like you!"

"She's a very clever girl," Annie told them. "I bet you could teach her lots of tricks."

Naima could barely take her eyes off Suzy as Annie led them outside to give the little puppy a run around in one of the exercise paddocks. They played doggy-in-the-middle, throwing a gold squeaky toy to each other, with Suzy happily barking and racing after it, her tail wagging happily.

After a while, Dad pretended to throw the toy to Naima, and Suzy shot towards her.

"I haven't got it," Naima told Suzy, as she rushed up to her, barking excitedly. Naima dropped to her knees to stroke the puppy's curly ears. Suzy cocked her head on one side, then trotted back over to Dad. Dad showed her the toy and her tail wagged fiercely. Then he pretended to throw it again. "Dad!" Naima complained. "Don't tease her!"

But to her surprise, this time Suzy just stared at Dad, then ran round to where he was hiding the toy behind his back. She jumped up at his hands and gave a high-pitched little "Yap!"

"Clever girl!" Dad grinned, giving her the toy. Suzy picked it up in her mouth and scampered over to Naima. "She's one smart puppy!" Dad smiled.

"She's *perfect*!" Naima said, bending down to give the little dog a hug. Suzy curled up in her lap, the toy in her mouth. "Oh please, please can we get her?"

Naima looked up at Mum and Dad hopefully. Suzy looked up at them too, a pleading look on her face.

"Looks like we've found our puppy." Mum grinned.

"Yes!" Naima hugged Suzy close and kissed her furry head. "Welcome to the family," she whispered.

Tween Time

As they got in the car, Mum, Dad and Naima were all talking excitedly about Suzy. While Mum and Dad had gone to fill out the paperwork to make Suzy properly theirs, Naima had helped Annie take her back inside and said a sad goodbye to the little pup. It would be a couple of weeks before Suzy could come home with them, because someone from

Battersea would have to come and visit the house first and check that it was a nice, safe home for a new puppy.

Suzy had whined as Annie put her back in her kennel, and Naima had felt really bad about leaving her. "Don't worry, Suzy," she'd whispered. "We'll be back really soon, and next time you'll be coming home with us."

Suzy put her paw up and Naima covered it with her hand. Somehow, Naima just knew the smart little puppy understood.

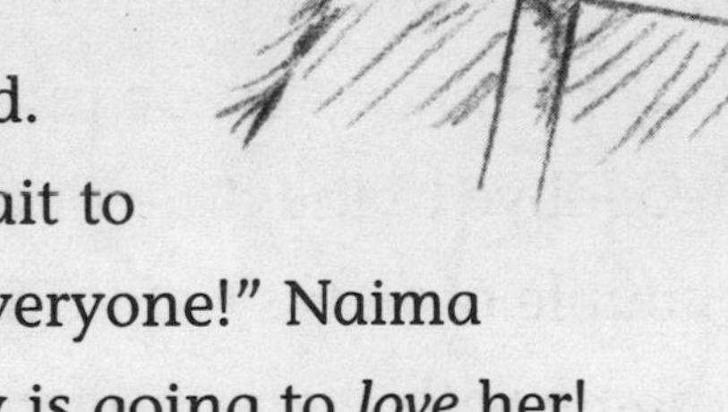

"I just can't wait to show her off to everyone!" Naima grinned. "Tammy is going to *love* her!

Can I call her now?"

"Sure." Dad smiled. "Just don't talk too long, OK?"

Naima dialled Tammy's number and waited impatiently while the phone rang.

"Where are you?" Tammy answered in a funny whisper.

"On the way home from Battersea," Naima explained. "We've picked our puppy – she's called Suzy and she's sooooo amazing. She's really smart and she's so cute!" Naima paused for breath.

"Naima!" Tammy whispered urgently.

"What?" Naima replied. Tammy didn't seem excited about Suzy at all – it was really unlike her. "Where are you, Tammy? You sound funny."

"Naima, I'm at the show," Tammy hissed. "For *your* audition! Everyone's waiting for you!"

Naima gasped. "Ohmygosh, the audition – I completely forgot!"

"Tween Time!" Mum yelled. Dad muttered under his breath and looked at his watch.

"It's OK, we can still make it," he said determinedly. "Can you reach your costume, Naima?"

"Yes," Naima said, patting the bag next to her.

"You'll have to get changed as we go along." Dad said. He pulled the car over and Mum jumped in the back next to Naima.

"We're coming, Tammy," Naima said as she hung up. Butterflies were fluttering in her tummy as Mum pulled her pink-and-gold costume out of the bag. She'd been thinking so much about Suzy that she'd completely forgotten about the audition. She started to take her jeans off and pull on her pink floaty trousers. Mum put a sparkly bindi in the middle of her forehead and brushed her hair as Naima struggled into her gold crop-top.

"I can't believe we lost track of time," Mum muttered through a mouth full of hairpins.

Naima couldn't either. She felt shaky and sick. She couldn't believe that soon she had to go and perform on stage in front of lots of people. The practise she'd done that morning felt like a long time ago. She couldn't even remember the first steps! Her tummy jumped, and for a horrible moment she thought she was going to be sick.

"Mum," she gasped. "I don't feel very well—"

"Stop the car!" Mum yelled.

*

"I'm sorry," Naima sniffed later that evening. She was tucked up in bed in her favourite pyjamas and felt fine now. But she couldn't help a tear rolling down her cheek as she thought about how Mum had made the call to the Tween Time organisers, telling them Naima wouldn't be able to perform. Everyone had been really nice about it, but it didn't change anything. She was out of the contest.

"Hush," Mum kissed her forehead. "You didn't have enough time to prepare, that's all, so you got a bit of stage fright.

It's fine. We'll make sure you're really ready for the next competition. I bet it happens to all the big stars, too."

"Even Beyonce," came a voice from the doorway. Mina was home from her party, looking tired but happy. She came and sat on the edge of Naima's bed and gave her a hug.

"Even Beyonce?" Naima giggled.

"Of course." Mina smiled and got under the covers with Mum and Naima, like she used to when they were little. "So, tell me all about Suzy."

Naima was just describing her silky fur when there was an excited "Whoop!" and they heard someone running up the stairs.

"Guess what, Nai?" Dad beamed as he burst into the bedroom. "You're still in! That was the Tween Time organisers and they said that because you've performed so well in the past, they'll give you a place in the Tween Time competition next month! They're giving you a second chance! Isn't that great news?"

"Great!" Naima smiled weakly but she felt a nervous flutter inside. It wasn't dancing that had given her stage fright, it was doing the routine all on her own. And that would still be the same in a month's time. She was going to get sick and ruin it all over again!

Home Sweet Home

Naima pressed a button and the familiar music filled the room. She took her starting position, standing with her legs crossed and her hands pressed together over her head.

Over the last couple of weeks she'd rehearsed every day after school, and she was feeling a bit better about the performance. It wasn't as much fun without Mina though. A few days ago she'd been practising her routine in the lounge when a lady from Battersea Dogs & Cats Home had come and checked the house. She'd told Mum that it would make a lovely home for a puppy, and said that they could come and pick Suzy up whenever they were ready.

Naima was practising as much as she could now so that she could spend all her time with Suzy when she arrived. Dad had gone to pick her up after he finished work and Suzy was expected home any minute now!

When the last notes sounded, Naima sank to the floor with her hands fluttering over her head for the big finale. As she lay there she heard a car pull into the driveway. Without pausing, she jumped up and ran to the door. "Mum! They're here!" she yelled.

She ran to the front door, but someone else beat her to it. "Welcome home, Suzy!" Mina yelled, flinging open the door. "Oh Nai, she's absolutely gorgeous!" she squeaked as Dad walked up the driveway, holding Suzy's lead. The little puppy scampered around his feet, rushing from one interesting smell to the next, her eyes bright and excited.

"Hi Suzy," Naima called, "welcome home!"

"Stand back and let her in," Dad told her. "She needs to get used to her new surroundings." But Suzy rushed right up to Naima and jumped up at her legs. Naima knelt down and Suzy jumped all over her, licking every part of her that she could reach.

"Hold still!" Naima giggled as she tried

to unclip Suzy's lead. As soon as she undid it, Suzy padded off into the kitchen. Naima followed behind her. "Look, Suzy!" She pointed. "There's your bed, and your bowls." One of the bone-shaped bowls was already filled with water, and Suzy stepped straight up to it and started lapping it up, her little pink tongue darting in and out as she drank.

Then she went over to sniff at the empty bowl.

"I think she's hungry," Namia said.

"The puppy food's

in the cupboard under the sink," Mum told her.

Naima opened the cupboard door. Suzy trotted after her and bounced about happily as she recognised her food. She was so excited that she almost climbed in the cupboard as Naima got out a chicken-flavoured sachet for her. Naima rustled the packet as she walked over to Suzy's food bowl and Suzy barked excitedly, jumping up and down.

"That must be why she's called a *Springer* Spaniel," Dad laughed as she bounced up and down like she was on a spring. The brown lumps that came out of the sachet didn't look much like chicken, but Suzy seemed to like it. She put her nose in the bowl and started gulping it down. When she was finished she licked her lips and looked around, wagging her tail.

"Was that nice?" Naima asked her.

Suzy panted and trotted back out into the hall. Then she started scrabbling in a carrier bag.

"Looks like she's found her presents!" Mina laughed.

Naima opened the bag, and showed Suzy the shiny pink collar she'd chosen for her. It had gold letters attached to it that spelt out SUZY.

Suzy sniffed it and Naima quickly put it round her neck. "Sit still," she smiled as she did up the buckle. Suzy scratched at the collar with her back leg, turning it so that the letters were at the back of her neck.

"She wants everyone to see her name!" Mina grinned.

"I've just got one more thing for you," Naima said, looking down into Suzy's beautiful brown eyes. Naima's arms had already been full when she'd seen it in the pet shop, but it was so perfect that Mum insisted they bought it.

Suzy couldn't wait for Naima to give it to her. She dived into the plastic bag and pulled out a blue toy. It squeaked as she dropped it between her paws and she started chewing on it.

"Oh, it's a rosette," Mina laughed. "The kind you get when you win a talent show."

"Yes." Naima grinned. "Suzy, I award you first prize – in the perfect pet category!"

A New Double Act

"Yap!" Suzy barked as the doorbell rang. Naima heard her pattering along the hallway, and then she came into the kitchen where Naima was eating her lunch. "Woof, woof!" she barked again, looking from Naima to the front door.

"It's OK, Suzy." Naima laughed as she got up. "It's only Tammy. She's come round to play with you." She scooped

Suzy up so that she didn't run outside, and unlocked the door.

"Where's Suzy?" Tammy yelled excitedly as she burst in. "Ooohhh!" she squealed as she caught sight of the little dog in Naima's arms. She stroked Suzy's ears, and the puppy turned over to get her tummy rubbed.

Naima, Tammy and Suzy went out to play in the garden. They were racing around, chasing a ball, when Tammy suddenly stopped.

"Suzy follows every step you make," she giggled. "She's like a little furry shadow!"

Naima looked down at Suzy. Then she took a step to the left. Suzy copied. Naima did a little jump. Suzy leaped after her and sat waiting, her tongue hanging out. "Yip, yip, yip!" she barked, as if to say, "What next?"

"Pass me the squeaky toy," Naima told Tammy. "I want to try something." Tammy threw her the blue rosette and Naima waggled it in front of Suzy's nose. Then she moved it slowly forward, and Suzy trotted after it. Naima stood with her legs far apart and bent down to slowly weave the toy around her ankles. "She's doing it!" she whispered to her friend as the clever little pup followed it. "She's like the dogs on *Britain's Got Talent*!"

"She's so clever," Tammy agreed. "We've tried to train Archie to do lots of tricks and he can never do them. He's nearly twelve and he still doesn't know how to walk to heel. You've only had Suzy a day and she's following at your feet already!"

"She's a natural!" Naima laughed, bending down to gently ruffle Suzy's little ears.

"They always say that dogs are like their owners," Tammy said. "It seems Suzy likes performing as much as you do!"

Naima glanced from her friend to her puppy, who was waiting at her feet. "Tammy," she breathed. "That gives me the most brilliant idea!"

"Please, please, please . . ." Naima crossed her fingers as she looked over her mum's shoulder at the computer screen. As soon as Tammy's dad had come to pick her up, Naima had explained her idea to Mum, and she was now looking at the rules on the Tween Time competition website.

Naima squeezed her fingers together tightly as Mum scrolled down the list of rules.

"Competitors must be between eight and thirteen . . ." she murmured. "Must have own shoes and props . . . No, there's nothing here that says that you can't use animals in the act!"

"Yes!" Naima grinned. "So, can we?"

"You want to do your dance routine with Suzy?" Mum asked.

"Yes! She'll be brilliant!" Naima cried. She quickly showed Mum the moves she'd practised with Suzy in the garden, and Suzy performed them perfectly! When they'd finished, Mum glanced at Naima. Suzy put her front paws on Mum's chair and whined gently. "See," Naima added. "Suzy wants to too!"

"Well, it would certainly be an unusual act. And if it'd be more fun for you, my *beti* . . ."

Naima dropped to her knees and swept Suzy up in a hug. "Did you hear that, Suzy?" She smiled. "There's a new double act in town!"

"Woof!" Suzy barked happily.

Dress Rehearsal

Naima peeked out of her bedroom window as everyone settled down in the garden. She'd spent every spare moment of the past few weeks practising with Suzy, and it was almost time for the Tween Time competition. Suzy loved performing and thought it was all a big game. First Naima had got Suzy to follow the squeaky toy around, then she switched to using a treat, so the audience wouldn't see it. Every time Suzy got a move right Naima gave her a treat as a reward, and soon the routine was perfect. Suzy circled round Naima's legs while she shook her hips, and whenever Naima stepped forward Suzy put one of her paws forward too. The only thing that Naima couldn't work out was what to do for the big finish.

Yesterday Mum had been watching their progress. "You two look great. But it's a very different thing doing the routine here and in front of a lot of people. What we need is a dress rehearsal, with a real audience." Before Naima knew it, Mum had started calling everyone she knew.

Now, all her aunties and uncles and cousins and lots of friends were gathered in the garden. Mum and Dad had set out blankets for the audience to sit on, and there was a big patch of grass where Naima and Suzy could perform.

Naima looked in the mirror and checked her pink-and-gold costume. Then she bent down to tie matching pink and gold ribbons to Suzy's collar. Suzy wriggled as she attached them, and Naima felt butterflies flutter in her tummy. What if Suzy didn't like all the people watching – what if she got distracted and ran into the crowd, or forgot all her moves? And what if Suzy got stage fright like she had? Naima didn't want her little puppy to be scared.

She scooped Suzy into her arms and gave her a hug. "You're going to be great," she whispered into Suzy's fur. "You're the cleverest puppy ever." Suzy nuzzled up to Naima and gave a doggy grin.

Naima took a deep breath. "Come on Suzy," she whispered. "It's showtime!"

Naima and Suzy ran into the garden as the music started.

Naima had one of Suzy's treats hidden in her hand, and the others in a secret pocket in her trousers. As she did the first steps, Suzy followed her perfectly, then snuffled her little nose into Naima's palm to take her treat. She wasn't nervous at all! All Naima's friends and family cheered and clapped as they did the routine. They oohed when Suzy span in circles, and laughed when she ran through Naima's legs. Every time Naima looked at her puppy, Suzy's tail was wagging happily – she was having a brilliant time! Naima felt her heart swell with pride.

At the end, Naima lay on her tummy and fluttered her hands over her head.

She'd trained Suzy to lie down next to her, but instead the little puppy ran behind her. Naima kept a smile on her face. Suzy had done so well, it didn't really matter that she'd got it a bit wrong at the end. But then, out of the corner of her eye, she saw a flash of brown and white, and heard a gasp from the audience. Suzy had made up her own big finish and jumped right over her!

As soon as it was over, everyone crowded round to hug Naima and fuss over Suzy. As Auntie Asha stroked Suzy behind the ears, Mina came over to give Naima a hug.

"You were incredible!" She smiled. "I sort of wish I was doing it with you."

Naima grinned. "Well, Suzy is the perfect partner – much better than you!" she joked.

"Hey!" Mina laughed, then pulled Naima in for another hug.

Mum had made lots of food, and she'd even bought a special doggy dinner for Suzy. Soon the show had turned into a party! Finally Mum shooed everyone away, telling them that Naima needed to get a good night's sleep before the competition tomorrow – and Suzy too, of course!

As Naima got ready for bed she had butterflies in her tummy again – but because she was excited, not nervous. She couldn't wait to perform with Suzy tomorrow!

The Big Performance

"Wake up sleepyhead, it's the big day!" Naima opened her eyes to see Mum coming into her room with a tray full of toast and orange juice. There was a thump on Naima's tummy as Suzy jumped up onto the bed covers. "Good morning!" Naima smiled as Suzy came up to give her a good morning lick.

"Yap!" Suzy barked as Naima sat up.

"We've got to leave at ten," Mum said as she gave Naima her breakfast. "So you've just got time to get ready and have a quick practise." As Naima sat in bed and ate her toast, Mum started combing and plaiting her hair.

After one last practise run, everyone piled into the car. Naima carefully held

Suzy on her lap and brushed her fur until it was sleek and shiny. Suzy loved the feel of the brush and wriggled in her lap happily.

Naima could see Mum checking on her in the wing mirror and gave her a big smile. It was so different this time, she didn't feel scared at all. And it was all thanks to Suzy!

As they arrived backstage and Mum and Dad went to go and take their seats in the audience, Naima did feel a flash of nerves. But they went away when she saw how excited her puppy was.

"You're not nervous, are you Suzy?" she asked as the little pup jumped up at her legs with her tail wagging. "So I won't be either!"

"Next we have a very special double act – Naima and her Springer Spaniel, Suzy!" the announcer told the audience.

Naima put a big smile on her face and reached into her pocket for a treat. But they weren't there! Naima's smile disappeared, and suddenly she felt hot and panicky. The treats were still in Mum's handbag. And without them, Suzy wouldn't do the routine!

"Naima and Suzy!" the announcer said again, looking at where they were stood behind the curtain. When no one appeared, the audience started to mutter and talk.

Naima didn't know what to do. If Suzy didn't follow her, the whole act would be ruined. Everyone would laugh at them! She felt her eyes begin to fill with tears . . . but then she felt two little paws on her legs. Suzy was standing up on her back legs, looking up at her expectantly. "Yap!" she barked, then looked at the curtain as if to say, "Let's go!"

Naima gave a little laugh. "Are you ready to perform?" she asked. Suzy looked at the curtain and gave a whine. Naima stood up straight and wiped her eyes.

"OK," she whispered. "Let's do it. It doesn't matter if it all goes wrong, as long as we have fun!"

Naima pulled back the curtain and ran

onto the stage with Suzy at her heels. The announcer looked relieved. "Here they are!" he grinned. "Everyone, put your paws together for our next act – Naima and Suzy!"

The audience clapped as Naima took her starting position, standing with her legs crossed. The lights were so bright and hot that she could hardly make out the faces in the audience. Naima gave a big smile then she waved her hand, acting as if she was holding a treat. Suzy crossed

her front paws too.

"Ahhhh," the audience called.

Then the music started. After the first trick, Suzy nuzzled into Naima's hand for a treat and Naima held her breath. But Suzy didn't seem to mind that her hand was empty. She just carried on into the next move.

If you do this right I'll give you lots of treats when we get home! Naima thought.

The rest of the act went perfectly.

DOGS & CATS HOME

Naima was concentrating so hard that it felt like it went really quickly, and very soon it was time for the big finish. Naima knelt on the floor, fluttering her hands over her head. *Come on, Suzy*, she thought. Suddenly there was a cheer from the audience as Suzy jumped over her. Then another as Suzy jumped again! Naima couldn't help grinning. Her little puppy was a superstar – and a show off!

The audience went wild, cheering and whistling. Naima looked up to see them all standing up and clapping as hard as they could. She looked down at Suzy, tears in her eyes, and to her surprise Suzy jumped up into her arms! Naima couldn't stop grinning. This was the best moment of her entire life. She ran backstage, still holding Suzy, but the audience kept cheering so the announcer pushed them onstage again to give another bow. Then all the other acts joined them to wait for the judges to announce the results.

As she waited, Naima looked for her family in the crowd. Mum was crossing her fingers tightly. Naima really didn't mind what the judges said. She had Suzy, so no matter what happened she felt like she'd already won!

"As you know, today's winner goes on to perform on TV," the announcer said. "All the acts have been fantastic, but the judges thought that one was extra special. They've all agreed that the winners of the Tween Time competition this year are . . . Naima and Suzy!"

"Yap! Yap!" Suzy barked excitedly as Naima jumped in the air.

"We did it, Suzy, we won!" Naima yelled.

Mum, Dad and Mina rushed onto the stage as the announcer gave Naima a huge golden trophy. Naima bent down to show it to Suzy and the little puppy climbed up on her lap, then jumped inside! The audience cheered as Suzy peeked out from inside the award.

Naima lifted up the trophy with Suzy still inside it. "I could never have done it without you," Naima told her.

"Yap!" Suzy barked proudly.

"How do you feel about performing on TV?" the announcer asked, pointing a microphone at her.

Naima held the trophy tight as Suzy wriggled about inside it. Then Suzy sat down facing her, ignoring the crowd of people and looking up at Naima with her beautiful brown eyes. "As long as I get to dance with my puppy – I can't wait!" she grinned.

Read on for lots more . . .

🐾🐾🐾🐾

THE
DOGS HOM
BATTERSEA
PATRON -
ESTY THE QUEEN
AUSTIN

Battersea Dogs & Cats Home

Battersea Dogs & Cats Home is a charity that aims never to turn away a dog or cat in need of our help. We reunite lost dogs and cats with their owners; when we can't do this, we care for them until new homes can be found for them; and we educate the public about responsible pet ownership. Every year the Home takes in around 10,000 dogs and cats. In addition to the site in southwest London, the Home also has two other centres based at Old Windsor, Berkshire, and Brands Hatch, Kent.

The original site in Holloway

History

The Temporary Home for Lost and Starving Dogs was originally opened in a stable yard in Holloway in 1860 by Mary Tealby after she found a starving puppy in the street. There was no one to look after him, so she took him home and nursed him back to health. She was so worried about the other dogs wandering the streets that she opened the Temporary Home for Lost and Starving Dogs. The Home was established to help to look after them all and find them new owners.

Sadly Mary Tealby died in 1865, aged sixty-four, and little more is known about her, but her good work was continued. In 1871 the Home moved to its present site in Battersea, and was renamed the Dogs' Home Battersea.

Some important dates for the Home:

1883 – Battersea start taking in cats.

1914 – 100 sledge dogs are housed at the Hackbridge site, in preparation for Ernest Shackleton's second Antarctic expedition.

1956 – Queen Elizabeth II becomes patron of the Home.

2004 – Red the Lurcher's night-time antics become world famous when he is caught on camera regularly escaping from his kennel and liberating his canine chums for midnight feasts.

2007 – The BBC broadcast *Animal Rescue Live* from the Home for three weeks from mid-July to early August.

Amy Watson

Amy Watson has been working at Battersea Dogs & Cats Home for eight years and has been the Home's Education Officer for four years. Amy's role means that she regularly visits schools around Battersea's three sites to teach children how to behave and stay safe around dogs and cats, and all about responsible dog and cat ownership. She also regularly features on the Battersea website – www.battersea.org.uk – giving tips and advice on how to train your dog or cat under the "Fun and Learning" section.

On most school visits Amy can take a dog with her, so she is normally accompanied by her beautiful ex-Battersea dog, Hattie. Hattie has been living with Amy for three years and really enjoys meeting new children and helping Amy with her work.

The process for re-homing a dog or a cat

When a lost dog or cat arrives, Battersea's Lost Dogs & Cats Line works hard to try to find the animal's owners. If, after seven days, they have not been able to reunite them, the search for a new home can begin.

The Home works hard to find caring, permanent new homes for all the lost and unwanted dogs and cats.

Dogs and cats have their own characters and so staff at the Home will spend time getting to know every dog and cat. This helps decide the type of home the dog or cat needs.

There are three stages of the re-homing process at Battersea Dogs & Cats Home. Battersea's re-homing team wants to find you the perfect pet: sometimes this can take a while, so please be patient while we search for your new friend!

Have a look at our website: **http://www.battersea.org.uk/dogs/rehoming/index.html** for more details!

"Did you know?" questions about dogs and cats

- Puppies do not open their eyes until they are about two weeks old.

- According to *Guinness World Records*, the smallest living dog is a long-haired Chihuahua called Danka Kordak from Slovakia, who is 13.8cm tall and 18.8cm long.

- Dalmatians, with all those cute black spots, are actually born white.

- The greyhound is the fastest dog on earth. It can reach speeds of up to 45 miles per hour.

- The first living creature sent into space was a female dog named Laika.

- Cats spend 15% of their day grooming themselves and a massive 70% of their day sleeping.

- Cats see six times better in the dark than we do.

- A cat's tail helps it to balance when it is on the move – especially when it is jumping.

- The cat, giraffe and camel are the only animals that walk by moving both their left feet, then both their right feet, when walking.

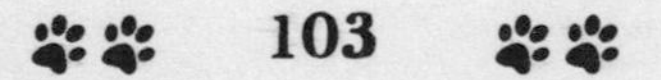

Dos and Don'ts of looking after dogs and cats

Dogs dos and don'ts

DO

- Be gentle and quiet around dogs at all times – treat them how you would like to be treated.
- Have respect for dogs.

DON'T

- Sneak up on a dog – you could scare them.
- Tease a dog – it's not fair.
- Stare at a dog – dogs can find this scary.
- Disturb a dog who is sleeping or eating.

- Assume a dog wants to play with you. Just like you, sometimes they may want to be left alone.
- Approach a dog who is without an owner as you won't know if the dog is friendly or not.

Cats dos and don'ts

DO

- Be gentle and quiet around cats at all times.
- Have respect for cats.
- Let a cat approach you in their own time.

DON'T

- Never stare at a cat as they can find this intimidating.

- Tease a cat – it's not fair.
- Disturb a sleeping or eating cat – they may not want attention or to play.
- Assume a cat will always want to play. Like you, sometimes they want to be left alone.

Some fun pet-themed puzzles!

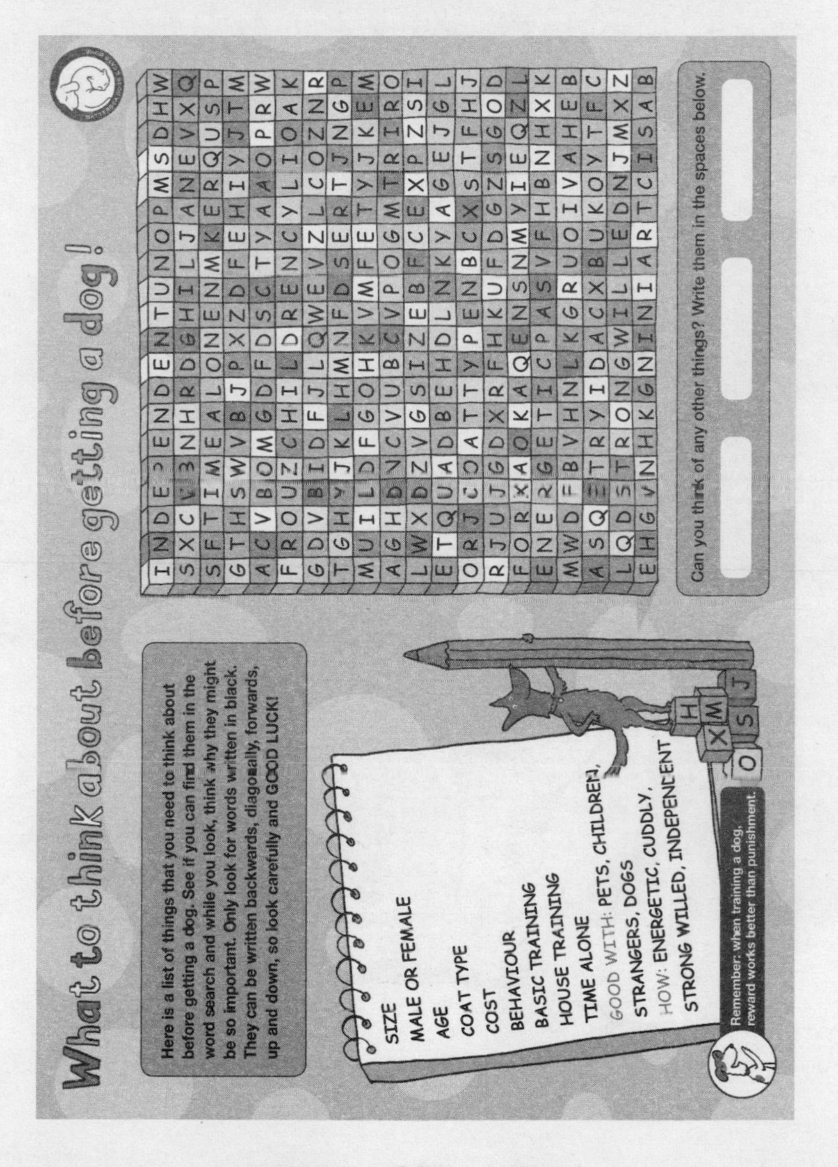

Tangled Leads and Crazy Maze
Oh dear! The Battersea staff are walking three dogs but the leads are tangled. Can you find out which dog belongs to which person by following the leads?
George
Michelle
Chris
Joe
Spikey
Sammy
Tessa
Start here
Who's walking who?
George is walking
Michelle is walking
Chris is walking
Remember: while in public all dogs must wear a collar and tag and should be kept on a lead.
Remember: always take a poop-scoop bag with you and clean up after your dog.
"Yummy yummy! Three big juicy bones for me," says Tessa, but can you help her find her way through the maze to find the bones?

Drawing dogs and cats

Here is a delicious recipe for you to follow.

Remember to ask an adult to help you.

Cheddar Cheese Dog Cookies

You will need:

227g grated Cheddar cheese
(use at room temperature)
114g margarine
1 egg
1 clove of garlic (crushed)
172g wholewheat flour
30g wheatgerm
1 teaspoon salt
30ml milk

Preheat the oven to 375°F/190°C/gas mark 5.

Cream the cheese and margarine together.

When smooth, add the egg and garlic and mix well. Add the flour, wheatgerm and salt. Mix well until a dough forms. Add the milk and mix again.

Chill the mixture in the fridge for one hour.

Roll the dough onto a floured surface until it is about 4cm thick. Use cookie cutters to cut out shapes.

Bake on an ungreased baking tray for 15–18 minutes.

Cool to room temperature and store in an airtight container in the fridge.

There are lots of fun things on the website, including an online quiz, e-cards, colouring sheets and recipes for making dog and cat treats.

www.battersea.org.uk